Joe Cocker Spaniel

Jen McVeity

Illustrated by Steve Axelsen

Supa
DooPers

sundance
A Haights Cross Communications Company

Published by
Sundance Publishing
234 Taylor Street
Littleton, MA 01460

Copyright © text Jen McVeity
Copyright © illustrations Steve Axelsen
Project commissioned and managed by
Lorraine Bambrough-Kelly, The Writer's Style
Designed by Cath Lindsey/design rescue

First published 1998 by
Addison Wesley Longman Australia Pty Limited
95 Coventry Street
South Melbourne 3205 Australia
Exclusive United States Distribution: Sundance Publishing

ISBN 0-7608-3291-9

Printed In Canada

Contents

CHAPTER I

Crash, Bang, Crunch.
Mary's Last Birthday Present

Mary Tilladay had a little turned-up nose and perfect dark curls and parents who had money. LOTS of money. That meant a tennis court in the backyard, long trips to Hawaii, and, every winter vacation, skiing for weeks and weeks at a time.

Every winter vacation, my parents took me camping by the lake. It usually rained. They had always promised to take me skiing—if I paid half the cost.

"Half!" I cried. "Where would I get that much money?"

"Get a job," said Mom. "You know. You work. You earn money. You go skiing."

For her birthday, Mary Tilladay got:
- one pair of the top in-line skates
- one portable CD player and seven CDs
- 47 birthday cards from friends, family, and kids at school who wanted to go to her party, and
- a dog.

Late on the afternoon of her birthday, Mary slung the CD player over her shoulder, put the skates on her feet and the dog on a leash, and went for a walk. Or a roll. The dog barked madly, jumped up on her, and wound the leash three times around her feet.

Crash, bang, crunch!

Mary Tilladay's last birthday present was a broken leg and crutches for six weeks.

9

That's how I got the job of walking Joe Cocker, her dog.

"He's a miniature cocker spaniel," Mary told me.

"Really?" I leaned against my bike and eyed him doubtfully. The thing looked more like a mad mop than a dog. It had stumpy little legs and a thick woolly coat.

"Arrf, arrf, arrf," it went. It was madly jumping up against my bike and me and Mary.

"Three dollars a day," I said. "I won't do it for less."

I'd only been at Mary's house for five minutes, and already the dog had put large, muddy paw marks all over my best jeans and just about chewed the tires off my bike.

"Two dollars," Mary said, "and the walk has to be at least half an hour."

Her mom and dad had made a fortune in business. I could see why.

"Okay. Two dollars," I sighed. How many walks with the mad mop did that mean? But winter was coming soon, and I needed to be on that mountain, skis on my feet and snow sliding full speed beneath them.

"Put the leash on him." Mary handed it to me like it was an order.

"Arrf, arrf, arrf!" If it were possible, the dog went even crazier, racing after its own tail.

"Arrf, arrf, arrf, arrf!" I was beginning to hate the sound already. I looked at the whirling back, the shaggy hair, and the stumpy legs. And then I opened my mouth and almost lost my first paying job ever.

"Of course," I said. "But which end is the head?"

CHAPTER 2

Walking the Mad Mop

Forget the tennis court and the trips to Hawaii. The very next present her parents should buy Mary Tilladay was obedience training for her dog—about five years' worth!

Those walks were the longest half hours of my life. Joe Cocker insisted on smelling every tree and bush and blade of grass.

He jumped up on fences, old ladies, and store windows. He deliberately tangled the leash around my feet, and he barked at just about everything on wheels—kids on in-line skates, bikes, parents with strollers, and even parked cars!

After ten days, I decided Mary should have supplied me with earmuffs!

"Arrf, arrf, arrf."

"Quiet, boy. Quiet. It's only a baby stroller." A mother gave me a dirty look and hurried on by, the baby suddenly squalling.

"Arrf, arrf, arrf."

"Down, boy. Down. That's not your ice cream." Two kids from school had to leap on their bikes and peddle away furiously, ice creams held high, while I dragged Joe back.

"Arrf, arrf, arrf."

The leash was tangled around my feet yet again. Joe was jumping up, trying to lick my face when, suddenly . . .

CHAPTER 3

The Chase, the Kick, the Fire Hydrant

WOOOOP! WOOOOP! WOOOOP! The noise of an alarm came blasting out of nowhere, wailing across the street. And out of nowhere, too, came a flying figure—a man flung open a gate, jumped the fence I was standing next to, and raced off down the street.

"GRRRRRRR!" With a huge growl, Joe took off after him.

"Joe!" I cried. "Joe, back! BACK!" I chased after him. And Joe chased after the man.

Somehow, in spite of those silly short legs, Joe was gaining.

"Stop, Joe! Stop!"

As I ran, I saw Joe lean forward and grab hold of the man's jeans with his teeth.

I was still running when I saw the guy lift his leg high—with Joe still attached—and swing it hard, very hard. Joe went flying across the pavement, skidded across the grass, and landed with a great thud against a fire hydrant.

"JOE!" I cried. "Joe!" I stopped running and knelt next to the tiny body. I picked him up gently and held him tightly.

In the distance, the alarm suddenly stopped.

My eyes watered, making it difficult to see.

In my arms, Joe opened his eyes and gave a tiny wriggle. For the first time in days, I wanted to hear him bark.

"Are you all right?" A lady was touching my arm, looking into my face. Her voice was somehow loud in the silence.

I nodded. "Yes, I think so." I looked down at Joe. He was panting and licking my face. Then he wriggled hard and broke free, and started jumping up on me.

"Arrf, arrf, arrf." I had to grin. "We're fine," I said again to the lady. "What happened?"

She smiled and straightened up, then helped me to stand, too.

"I'm not sure," she said, "but we'd better call the police. I think your dog has just taken a bite out of a burglar."

CHAPTER 4

A Hundred Questions and No Answers

"Was he carrying anything? Like a crowbar or a hammer?"

The policeman was tall, with an easy smile and a name tag that said Sergeant Rick MacDonald.

I shook my head. "No, I didn't notice."

I felt Mom squeeze my hand. She was sitting next to me on the couch. Dad was on the other side. Mrs. Tilladay was there, too, and Mary, of course, cuddling Joe Cocker and making a huge fuss over him.

"You're doing fine," Dad nodded at me. I sighed. I didn't feel like I had done much good at all.

Sergeant MacDonald had already asked about a hundred questions. "What was the man wearing? How old was he? How tall?" I didn't seem able to answer many of the sergeant's questions.

"What about his shoes? Were they running shoes, or boots, perhaps?" Sergeant MacDonald smiled encouragingly.

"Running shoes, I think . . ." I tried to remember. "I was frightened for Joe, you see, too frightened to notice things well."

The sergeant nodded.

"It all happened so fast. And then when he kicked Joe . . ."

I saw Mary shiver and put her face against Joe's furry head. She looked up, saw me watching, and smiled. I grinned back.

Suddenly I didn't feel so useless after all.

CHAPTER 5

One Tiny Fact and One Big Plan

Soon life got back to normal—and back to the daily walk with the wonder dog.

One day, after yet another hot, tiring, and embarrassing walk during which Joe never shut up, I told Mary, "You know, Joe really should go to obedience classes to get trained."

"Trained?" Mary asked. "Why?

I shrugged uneasily. I would have thought it was obvious. Joe might have been good at biting burglars, but the rest of the time he was just a plain nuisance.

"He barks at almost everything."

"Just things on wheels. He always has," Mary said.

"That means skateboards, trucks, cars, and baby carriages. Plus trains. And you can add fire hydrants to the list, too." She looked at me, puzzled. "Every time we pass one, Joe goes all stiff-legged and growls," I explained.

"Joe doesn't growl," she said. "He only barks."

"Wrong. He growls like crazy at the house that was robbed, and he goes bananas at another place down on Chapel Street. And just for good measure, he now hates male joggers." A couple of joggers had gotten a warning growl once or twice.

"It makes sense," she nodded. "He obviously remembers the burglary."

"Oh, yeah. Sure." How did you get through to this dog owner? "So why the house on Chapel Street?" I asked.

"It's strange." Mary was frowning. "Very strange." She gave me what was meant to be a meaningful look—only I didn't have a clue what the look was supposed to mean. I shrugged.

"Yeah, well . . . so, maybe some toddler left his tricycle out front," I said. "Or a whole group of joggers live there."

"Or one jogger. One man."

"One man?" I didn't follow her meaning.

"Yes." She gave me a look like if I had one more brain it would be lonely. "One man in running shoes and jeans. One man who has a habit of stealing!"

People didn't say no to Mary Tilladay very often. Maybe that's why she looked so surprised when I did.

"No," I said. "No way!" She wanted to come on the walk with Joe and me. More exactly, she wanted to go to Chapel Street.

Mary just looked at me, swung on her crutches, and waited.

"You can't be serious," I said at last. "So Joe growls at some house—so what! He barks at every second thing that moves!"

"Barks, maybe," she said, "but he doesn't growl."

"He does now. Joe growls at anything." I shook my head. "You've taken one tiny fact and made up a whole story about it. Get real. That dog needs obedience school—and fast!"

"What makes you the expert all of a sudden?"

"I walk the dog. I'm the one who needs earmuffs!"

She picked up her mom's cellular phone, put it in her pocket, and then swung on her crutches again.

"So, what are you planning to do?" I asked. "Go up and knock on the front door and ask, 'Are you a burglar?'"

"Something like that." She grinned.

"Your parents would kill us if they knew."

She shrugged. The thought didn't worry her at all.

"You don't even know what the guy looks like." I kept on trying.

"No, but you do. And you'll be hiding in the bushes, watching."

"Okay. Fine. Sure." I was losing this battle, and I knew it. "But if I'm right and you're wrong, Joe goes to obedience school. Right?"

"Right." She smiled.

CHAPTER 6

A Stroll Along Chapel Street

I didn't like it. I didn't like it at all when Mary swung along on her crutches all the way to Chapel Street, Joe dancing around her, tangling her in the leash, and just about breaking her other leg.

I didn't like it when she swung herself up the path of the suspicious house with a book of raffle tickets she was going to pretend to sell.

And even though I knew she was wrong, I didn't like hiding in the bushes while she walked right up to the front door of the house and rang the bell. The hairs on the back of my neck tickled and prickled. I didn't like it at all!

Dark hair, a black windbreaker, a wide nose. The guy who came to the door didn't look familiar. But then, I could hardly see a thing, there were so many branches in my face.

" . . . to buy raffle tickets," Mary was saying to him.

"Raffle tickets?" The voice didn't ring any bells either. But then, the real burglar had been too busy running to talk to me. I eased back a few branches and craned my neck, trying to see. He wore jeans—that was a start—and running shoes.

"To help our school buy playground equipment." Mary was waving the book of tickets under his nose.

"Sorry." He didn't sound at all sorry. But then he didn't sound like a burglar, either. He stepped back and started to close the door. Did I know him? Did I? Mary would kill me if I couldn't say. I grabbed leaves in both hands and peered out frantically.

"Arrf, arrf, arrf!" There was a blur and a noise, and a fast-moving mass of white fur went tearing down the path.

"GRRRRRRRRRRRRRRRRRR!"

"Joe!" cried Mary. She tried to grab him.

But Joe had his teeth sunk into a familiar pair of jeans and was not letting go.

"Get off!" The man lifted his leg and shook it.

"Stop it!" I knew what was going to happen next. I recognized the man now. That leg, that movement. I raced to the front step. "Stop!"

But I was too late. The man lifted his leg high and swung it hard. For the second time, Joe went flying through the air, legs scrambling madly.

And the man was off, racing down the street, running for dear life. I recognized him for sure now. Knew that run. I made a grab for Joe and held him tightly. We didn't bother to give chase. What for? We now knew what the thief looked like, what he was wearing, and exactly where he lived.

CHAPTER 7

Joe Cocker, Wonder Dog

"We don't often make an arrest on the evidence of kids as young as you two," said Sergeant MacDonald. He was sitting in our living room with another police officer, and he was smiling even more widely than the last time.

"So he really is the burglar?" asked Mom. She looked as if she couldn't believe it.

"He certainly is," the sergeant nodded.

Even before the thief was out of sight,
Mary had dialed the police station on
her mom's cellular phone.

A search of their computer files showed
that the house on Chapel Street belonged
to a man named Frederick Mantal, who
had a long record of arrests for burglary.

A search warrant had been issued. The police arrived at Chapel Street to find Mantal packing a suitcase, surrounded by about twenty computers—each stolen in recent burglaries.

"But what made you go there?" Dad was still looking stunned. "What made you knock on that door?"

I looked at Mary. She looked at me. I shook my head hard, meaning "Don't tell!" She ignored me—as usual.

"It was Joe," she said proudly. "He knew. He was growling at the house. He knew that the thief lived there."

"You mean . . . " Sergeant MacDonald had stopped smiling. "You mean it was the dog . . . ?"

"Well . . . "

"No!" He suddenly held up his hand. He looked a bit worried. "No, don't tell me. I really don't want to hear that a dog just solved our biggest burglary case this year!" He walked over to Joe. He was smiling again. "Thanks, wonder dog," he said, and reached out to pat him.

"GRRRRRRRRRRR!" Joe sat up, stared straight at Sergeant MacDonald, and growled. "GRRRRRRRRRRR!"

"Quiet, Joe. Quiet!" Mary tried to shut him up. It didn't work. I could have told her that.

"GRRRRRRRRRRRRR!" went Joe. He was giving the potted plant a warning now, all stiff-legged and serious. I looked at Mary. She was turning red.

"GRRRRRRRRRRRRR!" Joe was growling at the radiator. I was trying not to laugh.

"Next week," I said to Mary. "Obedience school. Right?"

Mary was bright red now. "Er . . . right," she said.

Jen McVeity

Jen McVeity lives in Melbourne, Australia, with one husband, two children, one cat, and no barking dogs whatsoever. Her kids often give her ideas for books—and then criticize the resulting stories ruthlessly.

With over twenty books published, Jen likes to create stories that make people laugh or cry—sometimes both at the same time.

Jen has jumped off cliffs, skied glaciers, swung on a circus trapeze, and traveled the world five times. She calls this research for her writing. Her family calls it having a good time.

Steve Axelsen

I was born and grew up in Sydney, Australia.

In 1973, I earned a B.A. in Sociology. After a brief period of house painting, I gradually found work as an illustrator of children's books, and I've been working in this field since 1974. Interestingly, I have never studied art formally.

I now live in the countryside with my family—my wife, my son and daughter, and my cat and dog. My hobbies include gardening and fairly frequent dog-walking.

My full-time work is illustrating for children. In particular, I do a lot of illustrating for educational publishing houses.